CLOUDY
with a chance of
MEAT BALLS ™

Junior Novelisation

by Stacia Deutsch and Rhody Cohon

SIMON AND SCHUSTER

London   New York   Sydney   Toronto

Read the original book by
Judi Barrett and Ron Barrett.

SIMON AND SCHUSTER

First published in Great Britain in 2009 by Simon & Schuster UK Ltd
1st Floor, 222 Gray's Inn Road, London WC1X 8HB

Originally published in the USA in 2009 by Simon Spotlight,
an imprint of Simon & Schuster Children's Division, New York.

A CIP catalogue record for this book is available from the British Library

ISBN 978-1-84738-660-1

Printed by CPI Cox & Wyman, Reading, Berkshire RG1 8EX

10 9 8 7 6 5 4 3 2 1

Visit our website: www.simonandschuster.co.uk

Prologue

Flint Lockwood was born on a small island in a sardine-canning town called Swallow Falls. When Flint was young, he was aware that there was something different about him. Unlike his parents and their neighbors, Flint had no interest in sardines. Instead, Flint loved to invent things, and he knew, without a doubt, that someday he would make something great.

Flint began inventing when he was in elementary school. He would never forget the day his teacher asked, "Did anyone remember to bring in a science project?" Flint's hand popped up in the air. He couldn't wait to show off his very first invention.

"Go ahead, Flint," the teacher said. Those were magical words. Flint hurried to the front of the room.

He firmly believed that he had discovered something that would change all their lives—forever.

"What is the number-one problem facing our community today?" Flint asked his fellow students.

They all looked at him blankly.

"Untied shoelaces," he informed them excitedly.

The children immediately glanced down at their own shoelaces, all untied, then looked back up.

"I have invented a laceless alternative foot covering: Spray-On Shoes." He raised a spray can up high for everyone in the room to see. Flint then held the can over his own bare feet, pressed the button, and within seconds, shoes appeared.

The classroom kids were impressed with the Spray-On Shoes—all the kids, except Brent, who was always badgering Flint. Brent had been a local celebrity since he appeared on sardine cans and commercials as a baby.

"How're you gonna get 'em off, nerd?" Brent challenged.

It was a problem that Flint had not thought about. He had been so busy getting the Spray-On Shoes to stick to his feet, he'd forgotten to consider how he was going to get them off. Flint bent low and tugged at the right shoe. Then the left. He tried the right one again. They wouldn't budge. He tugged and strained, but the shoes would not come off.

Brent began to chuckle. As young Flint struggled to remove the shoes, the classroom kids began to snicker along with Brent. It wasn't long before their mocking laughter filled the room.

"What a freak!" Brent exclaimed. "He wants to be smart, but that's lame!"

When Flint went home that day, he felt sadder and more depressed than he'd ever felt before. His invention was a failure.

Flint sat in his room that night, wondering what had gone wrong. Holding back tears, Flint attempted to bite the Spray-On Shoes off. When that didn't work, he used a screwdriver, but it broke. The scissors he borrowed from his mother bent around his foot. A handsaw turned to dust. A cinder block broke in half.

It was useless. The shoes were forever stuck to his feet.

His frustration and sorrow grew until Flint was forced to recognize that no one in the world really understood his drive to be an inventor. No one really *knew* him. Not his teacher. Not the kids at school. Not even his own father.

Flint's parents stood in the hall, right outside his

closed door. "Not every sardine is meant to swim, son," Tim, Flint's dad, called out through the thick wood.

"I don't understand fishing metaphors!" Flint cried, then flopped onto his bed.

Tim and Fran looked at each other. "Don't worry," Fran told her husband. She tucked a big box under her arm and gently knocked on Flint's door.

There was no answer, but Fran walked in anyway. Flint was sprawled out on the bed. Fran sat down next to him, and gently ruffled his hair. "Honey, I think your shoes are wonderful."

Rolling over, Flint looked up at his mother. "They don't come off. Why can't I make something that everybody likes? I'm just a weirdo."

Fran pointed around the room. On every wall were posters of great inventors. "Well, people thought these guys were weirdos too, but that didn't stop them," she said. Fran handed Flint the box she was holding. "I was saving this for your birthday, but . . . here."

"A professional-grade lab coat!" Flint exclaimed when he opened the box. Instantly feeling better, he jumped off the bed and slipped on the coat. It was way too big, but that didn't matter. "It fits perfectly," he told his mother.

6

"The world needs your originality, Flint," Fran said, admiring her son. "You just have to grow into it. If you keep inventing, I just know you're going to do big things someday."

Energized, young Flint rushed out of his room and up to his tree house where he worked on his inventions. With his mother's understanding and support, he knew that someday he was going to invent something really great.

Chapter 1

As the years passed, the town of Swallow Falls fell on hard times. The famous Baby Brent Sardine Cannery closed its doors shortly after everyone in the world realized that sardines were supergross. Many people in town lost their jobs and all anyone on the island could afford to eat were smelly, oily, leftover sardines; poached, fried, boiled, dried, candied, and juiced.

It seemed everyone had given up hope. Everyone except Flint Lockwood.

Flint was still hard at work, trying to invent something that would change the world. While walking through his futuristic lab toward his computer, posters of great inventors caught his eye. These were the same posters that had hung in his bedroom fifteen years earlier.

"I am on the verge of my greatest invention," Flint told his best friend and trusted colleague, a monkey named Steve. "One that will feed all of our hunger. A machine that will turn water into food." The monkey was wearing a thought-translator contraption that turned monkey thoughts into words. "Steve, can I count on your help?" Flint asked.

Steve looked up from the empty sardine can he held in his monkey hands and said, "Can."

"I knew I could!" Flint exclaimed. Flint pointed at a red button that was prominently displayed in the center of an elaborate computer console and declared, "Button on."

Steve nodded.

"Commencing tape." Flint watched as a reel-to-reel recorder fired up. "Blueprints complete!" he announced after reviewing the drawn documents. Flint then created a contained nuclear explosion. "Begin nano-mutation." He lowered a disco ball into a microwave. "Radiation matrix secure."

Those tasks finished, Flint proclaimed, "Computer boot!" Digital lines appeared across the computer's screen. "Visual enhancement complete!"

He and Steve took a quick break before Flint set up the Dangeometer. Flint knew that he'd have to watch it

9

carefully for any signs of trouble. His eyes were bright with anticipation as he announced: "Networking power grid!"

Flint slowly poured water into the top of his creation. "Beginning conversion of water into food." The air was electric. "Hydrating protein matrix." The machine glowed. "Calibrating flavor panel." Flint tightened a screw on the bottom of his device. "Priming chow plopper."

Success was within Flint's reach. With a click of the mouse, a recipe appeared on the computer screen. The same recipe showed up on the monitor of the new food machine. Flint took a deep breath, then announced, "Uploading recipe." He clicked the mouse again. The machine immediately voiced: "Cheeseburger."

Flint grinned. "Everyone is going to love this," he declared.

Flint watched as the chow plopper bulged bigger and bigger. . . .

A display read: MOLECULAR RECOMBINATION 60%, then changed to 70%, then 80% . . . 90% . . . and then, just as the display read 100%, a huge spark lit up the room!

That single spark started a chain reaction, which

quickly grew and grew into a small fireball. There was no stopping it. The spark traveled through the cables and out the laboratory.

Bang! Slam! Crash! Pop!

Across the yard, in the main house, all of Flint's father's appliances exploded at once in an incredible fiery eruption. The power went out and everything faded into blackness.

"Flint!" Tim shouted out his back door.

"Sorry, Dad!" Flint grabbed his tools and quickly hurried toward the lab exit. On his way out, Flint passed Steve. The monkey was busy banging a pipe against a metal bucket.

"Steve, keep working," Flint said, and then, humming an imaginary hero's soundtrack, Flint passed through a vaultlike door that opened to reveal an elevator. Flint jumped in.

"Whoosh." Flint mimicked the sound of the elevator's movement as it traveled down a shaft. An air-pressurized tube dropped the elevator down, under the ground, and then popped it up again into a Port-a-Potty outside Flint's father's house.

Flint rushed into the house and began fixing the blown fuses. "Re-energizing power unit," he muttered to himself. After a minute of twiddling around with

11

the fuse wires, the lights flickered a few times, then finally stayed on.

When Flint was done, he turned around.

"Yah! Jeez!" Flint was so surprised to find his father standing behind him that he smashed his head into the fuse box. The impact caused sparks to fly, which very nearly set his hair on fire. Gathering himself together, Flint mumbled, "See you, Dad!" over his shoulder, as he scurried back toward his lab.

Tim followed Flint out into the yard, saying, "Flint . . . um . . . uh . . ."

Flint knew what his dad was going to say. He'd heard the lecture a thousand times already. *Sigh.* Resigned to hearing it all again, Flint stopped.

It came as no surprise when Tim said the same thing he always said: "Don't you think it's time to give up this inventing thing and get a real job?"

Chapter 2

"Dad, inventing's the only thing I've ever wanted to do my entire life."

"I know that," Tim said in a firm voice, "but, all your technology stuff, it just ends in disaster."

"That is completely untrue," Flint replied, but even as he said it, Flint knew his father was right.

There had been the Remote Control Television he'd created when he was young. Unfortunately the whole contraption had gone batty. The TV kicked down the front door, fled the house, and ran off into traffic, frightening pedestrians.

The Hair Un-balder was another early invention that had had terrific potential. Flint convinced Tim to test the tonic. Very cautiously, Flint poured the Hair Un-balder onto his dad's bald head. The hair started to fill in nicely, but within seconds, Tim's new hair went crazy, growing uncontrollably into an incredible plume.

His next dream had been to build a Flying Car. A crowd gathered for his big test run. The car engine fired up, just like it was supposed to. The wings unfolded, just like they were meant to. And the car lifted off the ground as planned.

Things were going swimmingly until the car got caught in some low-hanging power lines. The fireworks were bigger than anything anyone had seen on the Fourth of July! The car rose over the pier and dove into the ocean, and the crowd ran off screaming in fear.

Flint hadn't invited anyone to see the test run for his next invention. Instead, he took the Monkey Thought Translator to his dad's bait-and-tackle shop. There were only a few customers in the shop when he'd arrived, just the right number for a test audience.

Flint introduced Tim to Steve and explained how the headband around the monkey's forehead worked: Whatever Steve thought, the Translator would turn into words that people could understand. When Flint flicked on the device, the contraption worked like a charm.

"Hungry!" Steve shared his first thought aloud. Everyone in the shop heard the monkey's thought—loud and clear.

Flint was thrilled. His first flawless invention! It was perfect! "How wise–," he began, but Flint's sentence was cut short by Steve speaking through the Thought Translator again.

"Hungry-hungry-hungry-hungry!" Steve repeated, jumping up and down. He might have been able to speak, but he was still a monkey, after all. Steve began swinging from the ceiling, as if he were in the jungle.

"No, Steve! No, no, no, no–," Flint yelled, but Steve was not about to be stopped. The monkey went on a rampage, knocking over shelves. Sardine cans fell and rolled everywhere. The few customers in the store rushed for the door. When Tim tried to stop the monkey, Steve pulled off a chunk of his mustache. So much for *that* invention.

Flint's Ratbirds came next. The plan was to gradually introduce the hybrid creation of a part rat/part bird creature into nature. It was a solid concept and would have worked—really, it would have—had the wild things not escaped their cages. The new breed swooped into town with a fury, terrorizing everyone they encountered.

Having fully considered his previous inventions, Flint was willing to admit to Tim that there had been a few small problems. "Okay," he confessed to his dad, "the Ratbirds, yes, they escaped and bred at a surprising rate, but I took care of that problem and disposed of them."

Just as Flint finished his sentence, Tim saw three Ratbirds descend, pick up a kid, and fly away with him. Tim shook his head, knowing that Flint had too much heart to actually destroy the Ratbirds. Instead he had simply moved the creatures to a swamp on the far side of town.

"Flint," Tim told his son, "you don't keep throwing your net where there aren't any fish."

"What?" Even as an adult, Flint had trouble understanding Tim's fishing metaphors.

Tim came right to the point. "I want you to work full-time at the tackle shop."

"The tackle shop?" Flint said, horrified that sardines might be his fate. He knew he was destined for more than sardines. "Aww, Dad. No!"

"Tackle is a good career," Tim told him.

"But you–," Flint tried to argue.

"I worked with my dad in the tackle shop," Tim countered.

As Flint begged his dad to reconsider, Steve climbed up onto Tim's head. Tim squirmed uncomfortably, trying to get the monkey off.

"Please, I'm so close with this one." Flint told his dad the basics of his newest invention. "I just have to hook it up to the power station and give it more power and it'll work. And it'll make all kinds of food, and then you could sell food in the shop, and everyone won't have to eat sardines anymore. It is going to be so awesome, Dad."

Steve jumped off Tim's head and Tim sighed. "Flint, you've got to start being realistic. I'm sorry, Son, no more inventing," he said firmly, before turning on his heel, ready to begin cleaning up the mess caused by Flint's latest explosion.

"Dad, I know I can do this," Flint insisted, blocking his dad's way back into the house. "And so did Mom."

By the look in his father's eyes, Flint knew that bringing up his mother was a huge mistake. Her death had been hard—for both of them—and Flint's dad dealt with it by not talking about it.

Tim looked sharply at his son, and then simply said, "Come on, let's open the shop." Flint knew that the conversation was officially closed. Without another word, he helped his father clean up.

Later that morning Flint looked on as Tim proudly unveiled a change to the sign in front of the shop. It now read: TIM AND SON SARDINE BAIT AND TACKLE.

"You feelin' it?" Tim asked.

Flint tried hard to sound enthusiastic, but all he could muster was, "Mmm-hmm . . ."

As Flint worked in the store, he had one eye on the TV that sat on the counter. The commercial that came on was an old one, from way back in those wondrous days when Swallow Falls had been the sardine-canning capital of the world. Flint sighed as he watched a baby tip over a wagon of sardines.

Flint mouthed the words along with the kids in the commercial. "Look out, Baby Brent!"

"Uh-oh!" Baby Brent replied. Those were the two words—sounds, really—that had sealed Brent's popularity as the island's cutest kid. Brent still lived off the fame of this commercial.

The announcer finished the commercial. "Baby Brent Sardines. Hand-packed in Swallow Falls."

Flint was about to turn off the TV when the mayor

of Swallow Falls appeared on the screen. "Freeze!" the mayor ordered, as if he knew what Flint was about to do. "We all remember our town's glorious past," the mayor said. "As your mayor, I hereby decree that our future is tourism!" The mayor was practically giddy. "That's why, without consulting anyone, I spent the entire town budget on the thing that is under this tarp. Which I will be unveiling today at *noooon*! Featuring a live appearance by Baby Brent himself!"

"Ugh." Flint finally turned off the TV and focused on stacking Baby Brent sardine cans in an odd tower shape.

Flint had been working at the shop all morning. He was wearing an apron boldly emblazoned with the words TIM AND SON SARDINE BAIT AND TACKLE on it. He looked like he belonged in the store, but his heart was still back at the lab, tweaking his water-into-food conversion invention and wondering how he could increase the power source.

A couple of old-timers, Joe Towne and Rufus, had come in and were hanging out in the shop. They weren't too happy that Flint was in the store, and wore annoyed expressions on their faces—until Brent came into the shop. Brent was no longer the cute baby in the old sardine ads. He was huge, out of shape, and looked like a slob in his tracksuit. But he still made everyone happy.

"Hey!" Joe Towne called out excitedly.

"Hey, it's Baby Brent!" Rufus said with a big smile.

"What is up, everybody?" Brent asked loudly, then turned to Flint. "Whatcha doing? Stacking cans with me as a baby on 'em?" he asked with a sneer. He showed off his famous Baby Brent pose before knocking down the tower of cans that Flint had been stacking. With a grin, Brent said his trademark line, "Uh-oh!"

Joe and Rufus whooped and hollered. For them, seeing Baby Brent in action was a thrill that never got old.

Unimpressed, Flint bent to collect the cans, at the same time muttering politely, "Hi, Baby Brent."

"Looks like the inventing career is working out superwell," Brent teased, handing Flint a runaway can. "Just kidding. It's not." He laughed at his own lame joke, then added, "Anyways, who wants to watch me cut the ribbon at the mayor's unveiling thing? I'll be using these bad boys to help save the town." Brent showed off a pair of huge golden scissors.

"Ooooh," said some of the shoppers.

"Boy-yo! See you, Flint. Sorry about your life not working out. I'm living the dream!" With that, Brent headed out, and everyone in the store followed, leaving Flint and Tim by themselves.

"You, uh, ready to shove off?" Tim asked. "Mayor's about to start that thing. . . ."

Flint really didn't feel like going over to the grand opening to see Baby Brent again, and he started to get an idea.

"You know, Dad," he said casually. "Why don't you go ahead. I'll hold down the fort here."

Not noticing that his son had other plans, Tim asked eagerly, "Really? You sure you can handle it?"

Flint smiled, really smiled, for the first time that day. "Yeah, Dad, I'm pretty sure I'll be fine."

Tim pulled on his jacket. "Huh. All right, then. I'll be back in half an hour, Skipper."

"Okay, bye." Flint shooed his father out the door.

A heartbeat after he was sure his father was gone, Flint looked around the shop. Everything would be fine. No one would be coming in, as they were all at the grand opening. And he would only be gone for a short while.

It was time to unveil his newest invention! Flint began to run, stopping only for a moment to throw off his apron and grab his lab coat.

Chapter 3

In Sardine Circle, the town center, excitement was brewing. People were gathering in front of a large stage that had been set up for the occasion. Behind the stage, the mayor was pacing, tense. Brent was with him.

"This town's too small for me, Brent," the mayor complained. "I want to be big. I want people to look at me and say, 'That is one big mayor.' That's why this has to work. It has to work! Otherwise, I'm just a tiny mayor of a tiny town full of tiny sardine-sucking knuckle-scrapers."

Brent looked up. He was eating sardines from a tin. "But not me, right?"

"Oh, not you, Brent, no," the mayor assured. "You've always been like a son to me."

Pasting a smile on his face, the mayor walked onstage. "Hey, hey, everybody!" he called out, as the small crowd cheered. "Under this tarp is the greatest tourist attraction ever built by humans!"

While the mayor spoke, Flint slipped undetected through the throng. He tiptoed toward the power station, his newest machine tucked under his arm. "It just needs seventeen thousand more gigajoules," Flint told himself as he snuck forward. "Go, go, go, go, go, go, go!"

"What are you doing, Flint Lockwood?"

Drat! Flint was caught by Earl, the town's overzealous cop who always played by the rules. Flint quickly shoved the machine behind his back.

"I'm just holding my hands behind my back respectfully, sir," Flint replied, anxiously looking past Earl at the power station. He was so close.

"You know what you are, Flint Lockwood?" Earl asked.

"No," Flint replied.

"A shenaniganizer! A tomfool!" Earl pointed to a boy standing nearby. "You see my beautiful angel son, Cal?"

"'Sup," Cal said with an attitude.

"I love him so much," the cop continued. "This

24

is my only son. I want him to have a bright future. A future in which you don't ruin our town's day with one of your crazy science doodley-bopper thingies."

"Well, you know, that's all behind me–," Flint replied slyly.

"I've got my eye on you," the cop warned.

From the corner of his own eye, Flint saw his chance to get away. He pointed across the street. "Oh my gosh, a jaywalker!" Flint shouted.

Within seconds, Earl was off and running after the jaywalker and Flint was back on track. He hurried toward the power station, with Steve hot on his heels.

The mayor, still onstage, was revealing how he'd spent the town's money. "I've arranged for live coverage from a major network and their most experienced professional reporter!" Little did he know that back in New York, the Weather News Network was preparing to send its new intern to cover the Swallow Falls event.

That intern was Sam Sparks. She was cute and young, and up until this very moment, her biggest task had been to deliver coffee. Sam would never forget the moment when the producer had said to her, "Intern, how would you like to do a weather report from a rinky-dink island in the middle of the ocean as a favor to my cousin?" Sam had been so excited that she spilled the coffee she'd been carrying.

The producer had partnered her with a cameraman named Manny and given them a weather van.

Sam couldn't stop gushing to Manny the whole way over to Swallow Falls. "Can you believe it, Manny? Temporary professional meteorologist!"

As they approached the island, Sam grew more and more nervous. "Manny, what should my opening be? 'Welcome, America, I'm Sam Sparks.' Or 'Hello, America, Sam Sparks here.' How about 'Oh, America, hi. I didn't see you there. It's me, Sam Sparks.'"

Sam was clearly on cloud nine. "Oh, Manny, I am finally on my way! Across the ocean!"

Back in Swallow Falls, Flint could hear the mayor prepping the crowd for the "big-time" reporter's arrival. "Now, when she gets here, I want to see a lot of smiling faces," he was saying. Flint half-listened to the mayor drone on as he crept past the power station's warning signs: DANGER! ELECTRICITY!

"This is a great idea," Flint told Steve as he grabbed a bunch of connector cables in one hand and began to climb the tower with the other.

In New York, the regular news anchor for WNN was prepped and ready to turn the broadcast over to his new roving reporter, Sam Sparks.

"Weather News Network," the anchor intoned, beginning his newscast the same way every time. "Weather news happens . . . or not."

The camera cut away to the WNN weather van, parked next to the stage in Swallow Falls. "Now we'll go over to Swallow Falls where our intern is on her first day on the job. Or should I say first *gray* on the job. Looks pretty cloudy there. Intern?" The anchor turned to Sam for her report.

The green light on Manny's camera came on, showing that Sam was now on TV—and she panicked. "Hello, Sam Sparks, I'm America. It's Swallow Falls degrees . . . and, uh, let's just go to the mayor."

Manny turned the camera and focused on the stage.

"Thank you and welcome, national television audience!" the mayor said as he launched into his welcome speech.

"And now, here to cut the ceremonial ribbon, Swallow Falls's favorite son, Baby Brent!" From behind the stage curtain, Brent appeared. And as he had done at many other public events, he dramatically ripped off his oversize tracksuit to reveal an enormous diaper underneath. The crowd broke into wild applause.

"He's still got it, folks!" the mayor announced.

Brent was all jazzed up. "Yeah! Hee-hee-hee! I'm the best person in the whole town!"

Brent then modeled his signature pose, before purposefully knocking over a wagon of sardine cans with his chunky arm. Then, like clockwork, he uttered, "Uh-oh!"

At the power station, Flint was busy connecting a string of jumper cables to the electrical tower. As he struggled to attach the final cable, Flint was zapped by a flying spark and was immediately knocked off the tower.

"Yahhh!" Flint cried as he fell.

A few minutes later Flint got up, slightly bruised but glad to be alive. He quickly checked his cables. One end still held tight to the tower, so he grabbed the other end and ran to his machine. Flint began to attach the clips.

That was when Earl sensed trouble brewing. "My chest hairs are tingling. Something's wrong," he said. Then, like an Olympic gymnast, Earl acrobatically flipped toward the power station.

In the meantime the mayor was about to unveil

his surprise. "So here it is, the attraction the whole world has been waiting for . . . SardineLand!"

Brent cut the ceremonial ribbon with his giant scissors. The tarp that hid the surprise slowly peeled away to reveal a small Sea World–like theme park.

The crowd clapped enthusiastically as the mayor pointed out the finer features of the amusement park. "Rides! And exhibits! And featuring Shamo, the world's largest sardine and his flaming hoop of glory!" Everyone crowded in to see Shamo, a tiny fish in a very large bowl, with a ring of fire to jump through.

The mayor joked, "Those of you in the splash zone, look out!" He winked at Joe Towne, who was sitting in the front row in the only seat marked SPLASH ZONE.

"Yeah!" the old man cheered.

Just as Shamo was being unveiled, Earl hurried out of Sardine Circle, toward Flint, yelling, "Flint Lockwood!"

Seeing the police officer headed his way renewed Flint's determination to get his machine working. He quickly attached the final cable and fired up the contraption. "Uh, just a second!" Flint called out to Earl. "I'm in the middle of a–yaaaa!" A superbright, incredibly strong spark from the electric tower sent the machine shooting off like a missile. Flint was

29

dragged behind, hanging on to the jumper cables for dear life.

"Aaaagghh!" he screamed again as he soared headfirst into Sardine Circle and straight into the crowd.

Meanwhile Sam continued to report on the day's event for her TV audience. "Well, looks like things in Swallow Falls are *sardine* to get better. For–"

Wham! Flint, flying at top speed, suddenly appeared and knocked Manny's camera into Sam. Not only did it startle her, but with the camera lens smooshed right up against her face, Sam now felt and looked completely ridiculous in front of a national TV audience.

"Aah, sorry!" was all Flint managed to say to Sam while the machine whooshed and zoomed around Sardine Circle, then crashed into the scaffolding that supported Shamo's fish bowl.

Flint desperately tried to stop, but it was no use. The machine banged past Tim, who scowled at his wildly flying son. It wasn't until Flint rammed into a stop sign and the jumper cables broke their connection that Flint finally crashed. The machine, however, kept on going. It shot straight up into the sky, disappearing like a rocket ship into the atmosphere.

Flint stared up after his invention. "No . . . ," he moaned, watching his life's work soar off into the clouds. But he had no time to dwell on this failure as Earl tackled him to the ground.

"You're under arrest, Flint Lockwood!" the officer declared, hauling Flint toward the squad car. "Thank goodness you only caused minimal damage to SardineLand."

Just then a rumbling began, growing louder and louder by the second. Flint and Earl turned to see the fish bowl scaffolding starting to give. Earl dropped Flint's arm and the two of them started to run.

Kraaak! The scaffolding broke through and the fish bowl toppled from its perch. Water splashed everywhere—everywhere that is, except on the actual splash zone. Safe and dry, Joe Towne complained, "Oh, come on!"

The large glass bowl began to roll, and by now, everyone was running. Brent was running too, still holding the ceremonial scissors. "I really shouldn't be running with these!" he commented to nobody in particular.

Flint spotted Steve in the direct path of the bowl. Flint stopped running, grabbed Steve, and then prepared for the worst. They were both surprised and relieved when the opening of the bowl rolled over them, leaving them completely unharmed.

After bouncing across a parking lot and causing a car to explode, the bowl was propelled up into the air. Shamo was thrown through the flaming hoop, out toward the ocean.

"Yippee!" Shamo exclaimed on his flight to freedom. He was, unfortunately, gobbled up the very next instant by a flying Ratbird.

Finally the bowl fell back down, landing upside down with a heavy thud on top of Flint and Steve! Trapped inside, Flint could see all the wreckage his newest invention had caused.

Outside the bowl, everyone glared at Flint. But the worst was when Flint caught his father's look. The disappointment in his face was crystal clear. Flint knew he had failed big-time. Again.

With despair, Flint slammed his head against the side of the fish bowl. *Craack.* The angry townsfolk watched as the bowl shattered, and Flint and Steve quickly escaped.

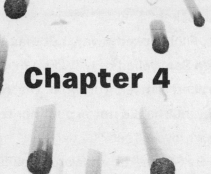

Chapter 4

After the SardineLand incident, Flint decided it would be better to stay away from the town for a while. He and Steve hung off a ladder at the end of the fishing docks.

At the sound of footsteps along the wooden planks, Flint pulled Steve back farther into the shadows. They heard a sigh. Then a microphone flew over their heads, and fell with a splash into the ocean.

Sam plopped down on the end of the dock and swung her feet over the edge.

"Ow!" Flint cried out as Sam hit him in the face.

"Oh my gosh, I am so sorry," she said, leaning over to see who was down there. "Are you okay? I didn't–"

"It's okay. It's just pain," Flint said.

"Sorry," Sam repeated. "I'm not myself today. My

whole career was ruined by some crazy jerk riding a homemade rocket."

At that, Flint looked away, but was sure he was caught when Sam yelled out, "Wait a minute!"

Flint braced himself for what the reporter was about to say, but he did not expect her to ask, "What is going on with your feet?"

"Spray-On Shoes," he answered, relieved that she hadn't recognized him. "They don't come off."

Reaching down, Sam grabbed Flint's foot and yanked it toward her. She was surprisingly strong, and had no problem holding him upside down.

"Cool!" Sam exclaimed, putting her face up close to the shoes. "This could solve the untied shoe epidemic." She thought for a second before asking, "What are they made of, some kind of elastic biopolymer adhesive?"

In that instant, Flint felt like he had been struck with Cupid's arrow. "Yeah, exactly . . . ," he said, suddenly smitten with someone who seemed to speak his language.

"I mean . . . ," Sam said, chuckling. "Wow, they're shiny." Then realizing she hadn't introduced herself, she said, "I'm Sam," before letting go of Flint's foot.

Flint's head immediately slammed into the ladder,

but he didn't seem to feel the pain. "Flint Lockwood," he said dreamily as he climbed up onto the docks.

Steve popped up and joined in the introductions. "Steve!" The monkey pointed to himself.

Sam was amazed. "Is that a Monkey Thought Translator?"

"Steve," the monkey repeated.

"Ha! Incredible!" Sam reached over to pet Steve. "Did you make this stuff?" she asked Flint. Then her expression changed. She jumped up and stood with her hands on her hips. "You! You hit me with the rocket!"

Poof! Flint's lovey-dovey dream shattered, and he snapped back to reality.

"You kicked me in the face!" he countered weakly.

"I said I was sorry!" Sam shot back. She turned away from Flint, furious.

Flint was about to argue with her when he was distracted by a loud *splat*. Some yellow goop landed on the water. Flint leaned over and scooped up some of the gunk. He was about to taste the stuff when—*plop!*—a pickle fell into the water.

Because her back was turned, Sam didn't see what was going on. Instead she was giving him a

35

piece of her mind. "Do you know how hard it is to break into the weather game? I spent my entire life building up to that moment. You get one shot at the show. And if you don't make it, it's back to cleaning the barometers. . . ."

Slam! Rattle! Something landed in a garbage can behind Flint. While Sam went on about her crushed reporter's dream, Flint peered into the garbage can. There was a slice of cheese inside. He reached for it, saying softly to himself, "Cheese?"

Suddenly a Ratbird appeared, startling Flint. It snatched the cheese and flew away.

"Whoa!" Flint exclaimed, suddenly realizing what might have happened. "But that could only mean . . ." *Crash!* A loud thunderclap made Flint look up at the sky—and gasp in shock.

Sam stopped mid-sentence, looked up, and also gasped in shock. Steve gasped.

All over town, people were turning to look at the sky, and they could not believe what they were seeing.

After a superlong, extra-breathy, shocked gasp, Flint announced, "IT'S RAINING CHEESEBURGERS!"

Steve jumped around. "Excited!" he yelled.

Flint started laughing uncontrollably as tasty-looking cheeseburgers floated down from the sky. He opened his palm and a burger landed in his hand. He took a bite. It was delicious!

"My machine works! It really works!" Flint said with his mouth full.

"Your machine?" Sam asked, looking up in awe. "Is that what that rocket was?"

"Uh-huh," Flint replied as he took another juicy bite. "Do you like it?"

Sam caught a burger and after one bite exclaimed, "I love it!" She giggled. "This is just amazing! Look at this," Sam said, twirling around in the cheeseburger downpour. "This is the greatest weather phenomenon in history!"

Flint was happier than he'd ever been in his whole life. "Hey, aren't you a weathergirl?" he asked.

Sam gasped . . . again. Then she sprinted into action and headed toward Sardine Circle. Flint followed. They found Manny hanging out at the weather van, eating a cheeseburger. "Manny, get your camera!" Sam ordered.

In New York, the WNN anchor touched his earpiece. "This just in," he relayed to his national viewing audience, "our humiliated weather intern is apparently back for more."

"Thanks, Patrick." The camera cut to Sam standing in the town center. Behind her, cheeseburgers were falling from the sky.

She was no longer nervous. Sam stood up straight and looked directly into the camera. "Okay, everybody. You are not going to believe this one, but I am standing in the middle of a burger rain. You may have seen a meteor shower, but you've never seen a shower *meatier* than this. For a town stuck eating sardines, this is *totally* manna from heaven."

As Sam reported, Flint watched the reaction of the townspeople around them. The crowd was going nuts for the cheeseburgers. Cal shoved one into his mouth and gobbled it up in two bites.

"This is going to be big!" The mayor declared, before stuffing three burgers into his mouth.

Sam continued her live report. "This food weather was created intentionally by meekish backyard tinkerer, Flint Lockwood."

Earl and everyone around Flint stopped eating.

"Flint Lockwood?" the policeman said in surprise.

Everyone turned to look at Flint. After everything that happened that day, Flint was a bit wary of being the center of attention, so he timidly waved. "Hi."

Earl, ever the gymnast, tucked and rolled over to Flint. Then, instead of congratulating Flint, Earl tackled him. "You're under arrest for ruining SardineLand."

Pinned beneath Earl, Flint raised one eye to see Sam standing over them. "Flint, those burgers were awesome! The producer called and he was all, like, 'Everyone loves that food weather.'" She imitated her boss's deep voice.

"Food weather," the mayor repeated, suddenly getting an idea.

"What?" Earl asked, getting off of Flint.

"This could be even bigger than SardineLand," the mayor said.

"Can you make it rain food again? Please?" Sam asked Flint.

"Well, I don't really know if I–," Flint said.

"Please, please, please, please," Sam begged. Flint looked at her. He was definitely smitten with her adorableness.

"Yes," he agreed. Then Flint got up and led the way to his lab.

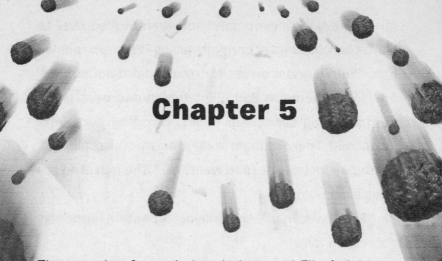

Chapter 5

The parade of people headed toward Flint's lab was intercepted by Tim. He wouldn't let Flint, Steve, Manny, or Sam get past him. "No," Tim said firmly, blocking the way to the Port-a-Potty.

Flint begged his father to move aside. "Dad, just give me one more chance!"

Tim looked sternly at Flint. "We both know that this was an accident."

"I know, but–," began Flint.

Tim interrupted. "Cheeseburgers from the sky, that's not natural."

"But my invention could save the whole town. You will be so proud of me, Dad." In a whisper, Flint added, "Plus there's a girl here. . . ."

Tim asked, "Can you look me in the eye and tell

me you've got this under control, and it's not going to end up in a disaster?"

Flint slowly raised his eyes to his dad's and quickly said, "Yes." He struggled to hold the gaze, however, and his eyeballs began to twitch. "I've-got-this-under-control-and-it's-not-going-to-end-up-in-a-disaster," Flint said as fast as he could, before he had to look away. Whew.

"All right," Tim said, backing away from the potty door.

"Thanks, Dad!" Flint opened the door for his guests. "So, Sam, this is where the magic happens." Flint, Steve, Manny, and Sam all smooshed into the Port-a-Potty.

Inside the elevator, Flint apologized. "Sorry about my dad. He's been like that ever since my mom died."

"Oh, gosh," Sam responded. "I'm so sorry. I didn't know—"

"I was super young . . . ," Flint paused. "I haven't really talked to a girl since then."

Sam blushed. "Oh, yeah. That makes sense."

"Hey, want me to guess your weight?" Flint asked innocently.

Sam tried to stop him politely. "No, that's all right—"

But Flint persisted. "I'm gonna guess about one . . . seven–"

"No, don't even finish!" Sam said, just as the elevator arrived at the lab. The four spilled out into the main chamber.

"Wow," Sam remarked, looking around. "You seriously spend a lot of time alone."

Flint laughed awkwardly, then he showed Sam a diagram of the food machine. "Here's how it works: Water goes in the top and food comes out the bottom."

"So when you shot it up in the stratosphere, you figured it would induce a molecular phase change of the vapor from the cumulonimbus layer?" Sam asked, poring over the details.

"That's actually a really smart observation." Flint replied, impressed.

Suddenly Sam got nervous. "I mean, the clouds probably have water in them, which I guess is why you shot it up there in the first place."

Flint was now nervous too. "Right, right, that's why I did that . . . on purpose."

"Right, yeah," Sam said, cautiously.

"Right." Flint looked down at his blueprint. "The machine uses a principal of hydrogenetic mutation."

He pointed to the picture of water molecules forming into hexagons from radiation waves. "Water molecules are bombarded with microwave radiation, which mutates their genetic recipe into any kind of food you want."

"So, pizza?" Sam asked.

"Yes," Flint replied.

"Mashed potatoes?"

"Yes."

"Peas?"

"Yes," Flint said smiling. "That's also a food."

Sam was thinking of all her favorite foods. There was a dreamy look in Sam's eyes when she asked, "Ooh . . . how about Jell-O?"

Flint grinned. "Do you like Jell-O?"

"I love Jell-O!" Sam exclaimed.

"I love Jell-O too. And peanut butter, right?" Flint asked.

"Oh, no, no. I am severely allergic to peanuts," Sam replied.

Flint desperately wanted Sam to like him, so he lied. "Yeah, me too!"

"So what's it called?" she asked.

"Peanut allergy," Flint said, distracted.

Sam smiled. "No, the machine."

"Of course." Flint snapped back into the conversation. "It's called the Flint Lockwood Diatonic Super Mutating Dynamic Food Replicator. Or the FLDSMDFR, for short."

"Fldsmdndffursur?" Sam tried to repeat.

Flint corrected her. "FLD. SM. DFR."

"Oh," Sam turned to her cameraman. "Manny, make sure you get this. He's going to make the food now."

Flint wasn't expecting this. "Uh, now? Uh . . . well, the thing is, I can't . . . wait to show you this hilarious Internet video!" He rushed over to his spare computer, successfully distracting Sam and Manny with an amazingly long YouTube video of a cat DJ playing "Fight the Power."

"It's so cute," Sam said, watching the cat spin the tune.

As Sam and Manny watched the video, Flint quickly rigged a remote control system using a satellite dish and a bunch of wires. He whispered to himself as he worked. "Pushing. Folding. Pressing. Taping. Turning. Painting. Switching. Staring. Motivating. Placing button."

He checked the Dangeometer. The meter was safely in the green zone.

Flint rebooted his main computer.

When the cat show was finally over, Sam said, "I can't believe I've been watching this for three hours!"

"I know!" Flint was furiously typing at his computer when Sam moved in behind him, still giggling about the video. The central screen now read: ENTER FOOD CODE.

"It's working," he said. Then, turning to Sam and Manny, he asked, "What do you guys want for breakfast tomorrow?"

Steve knew what he wanted. "Gummi bears," the monkey suggested.

"No, Steve, we both know how you get around gummi bears."

"How about eggs?" Sam asked.

"And toast?" Flint was prepared to create a full meal.

"Orange juice," Sam added.

"And bacon!" they said at the same time.

Flint eagerly typed on his keyboard:

```
food = <eggs>; then <bacon>(crispy); then
<toast> + <O_J>(nopulp); startclock <8:30AM>.
```

"So you're sure this is safe?" Sam questioned.

"Don't worry," Flint assured her. "I have a

Dangeometer that lets us know if the food is going to overmutate."

Sam looked concerned. "What happens if the food overmutates?"

Shrugging, Flint answered honestly, "I dunno, but that'll never happen." Flint pushed the send button. The signal from Flint's computer traveled up and out of the lab, past the Dangeometer, along the wires to the satellite dish, and into the sky.

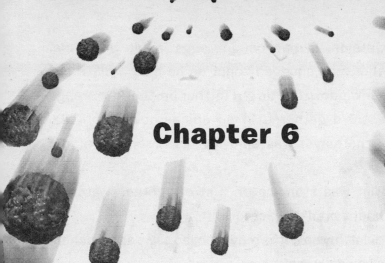

Chapter 6

Flint's FLDSMDFR floated peacefully among the clouds. At precisely eight thirty the next morning, fried eggs emerged from the clouds and began to descend toward Earth. A few minutes later bacon fell alongside the eggs.

Down below, in Swallow Falls, Sam was standing in front of a weather map, giving the morning's weather report. She pointed out various food symbols to her rapidly expanding national viewing audience.

"Well," Sam said, using a long pointer to indicate the small island. "Those cheeseburgers were only the beginning, because a breakfast system looks like it's on its way to Swallow Falls." She smiled, feeling at ease and clearly loving her job. "My forecast: sunny-side up!"

Outside, a man caught eggs in his briefcase. Another man snagged toast as he held a plate out his car window. A little girl fed her brother the orange juice she'd gathered in an upside-down umbrella. Even the mayor was enjoying his first meal of the day.

Flint was standing on a street corner, watching the happy breakfast-eaters.

"Flint, my boy," the mayor called as he approached. "Can you do lunch?"

Flint was happy to fill the mayor's request. He rushed to his lab, and at lunchtime it began raining sandwiches.

Comfortably holding two sandwiches in each hand, the mayor called Flint in for a meeting. "All right, here's the skinny," he began. "You keep making it rain the snackadoos and the weathergirl provides free advertising. I have taken out a very high-interest loan to convert this podunk town into a tourist foodtopia. All you have to do is make it rain food, three meals a day, every day, for the foreseeable future. And in thirty days we hold a grand reopening of the island as a must-see cruise destination, and everyone everywhere is going to love your invention."

Flint Lockwood had wanted to be an inventor ever since he was a young boy.

His dad, Tim, thought Flint should give up inventing and work at Tim's bait and tackle shop.

But Flint had a hunch that his latest invention—one that turned water into food—would be the biggest success ever!

And it was! Flint made food rain down from the sky every day.

Sam Sparks from the Weather News Network reported on the tasty weather.

The mayor and everyone in town couldn't be happier . . . until a spaghetti twister roared into town.

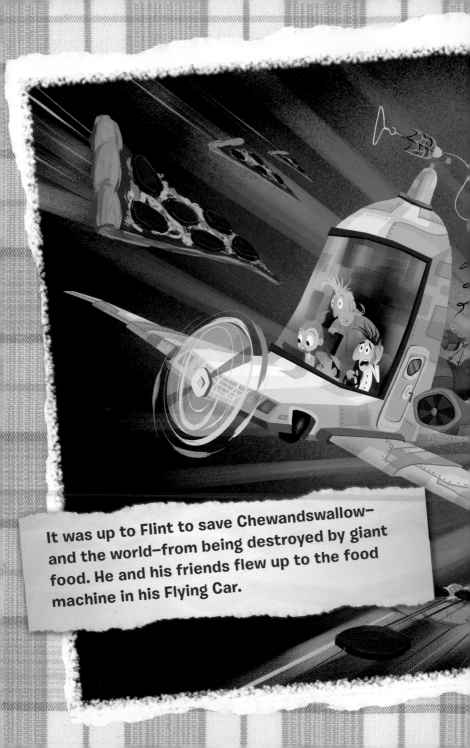

It was up to Flint to save Chewandswallow— and the world—from being destroyed by giant food. He and his friends flew up to the food machine in his Flying Car.

Flint's plan worked! And he was brought safely back to earth by his Ratbirds.

"You think so?" Flint asked. Maybe this *was* his big chance to finally do something great.

The mayor took a huge bite of sandwich before confidently declaring, "I know so."

The mayor was right. Everyone loved Flint's invention so much that they started requesting their favorite foods. After a meal was arranged, he'd tell Sam what was on the menu and she'd report it on TV.

The townsfolk were happier than they had been in years. The Baby Brent Sardines billboard was replaced with one for Flint Lockwood brand napkins, and the mayor even changed the town's name to Chewandswallow.

New industries were popping up all over town. The gas station became the place for antigas tablets. Stores started selling dental floss and bibs. A father and son created neck buckets to catch and carry the food. Abandoned buildings were repaired. The run-down city hall received a face-lift. The park was cleaned and flowers were planted.

On TV, Sam stood by a large pile of mixed food items, giving her report. "Leftovers?" Sam asked viewers. "Not a problem with Flint Lockwood's latest invention, the Outtasighter. So named because it catapults uneaten food *out of sight*, and therefore *out of mind*."

The Outtasighter was a fantastic contraption. A huge fork and spoon scooped up leftovers onto a giant plate. The plate dumped the scraps into a bowl at the back of the machine. With the pull of a handle, Flint and Steve showed people how to catapult their leftovers way into the distance, behind the dam at the top of the hill.

It didn't take long before tourists began coming to Chewandswallow, just like the mayor wanted. Flint was watching a group of foreigners as they walked past the main street shops, laughing and eating some falling food.

As the tourists wandered away, a sign in his father's shop caught Flint's eye. The sign that used to say SARDINES 10% OFF now read SARDINES 100% OFF.

Flint crossed the street and entered his dad's store. Tim sat alone at the counter, eating sardines from a rusty tin.

"Hey, Dad," Flint said. "I'm headed back to the lab. If you wanna come, I could show you how I make the food."

"Eh, no thanks," Tim said, popping a sardine into

his mouth. "That techno-food is too complicated for an old fisherman."

"Got it." Flint turned to leave.

"Could still use your help around here, though, you know." Tim pointed around the dusty shop.

"I have a job, Dad. Everybody's kind of counting on me."

"Right. Got it," Tim noted, and went back to eating his sardines.

A few minutes later Flint was in his lab, adjusting the antennae on the satellite when the doorbell rang. Police Officer Earl was at the door looking for Flint.

"Uh, it's my son Cal's birthday tomorrow," Earl said, "and I was just wondering if you could make it rain something special."

Flint squinted at the cop. "Well, I'm pretty backed up on requests. Plus you're always mean to me."

"It would just be one time," Earl said, clutching his hat nervously between his big hands. "For my special angel's special day."

Flint pursed his lips together. "I don't know. I should really let the machine cool down. . . ."

"Okay." Earl started to leave. "I knew it was a long shot. I just wanted Cal to see how much his father loves him. I thought you'd understand. You know how fathers are always trying to express their love and appreciation for their sons."

Flint let Earl get a few steps away, then called him back and agreed to help.

Back at his desk, Flint began to upload Cal's birthday surprise when he noticed that the Dangeometer needle was in the yellow zone. Flint tapped the needle and it settled back to green. Satisfied, he walked away. But the second he was gone, Steve tapped the needle, just as he had seen Flint do. And the needle popped right back into the yellow section.

The next morning, Cal woke up to a wondrous birthday sight. "Whoa!" he exclaimed when he opened his bedroom window. It was snowing ice cream!

"Happy birthday, Son," Earl said proudly.

"Dad?" Cal realized that the amazing weather was a birthday present.

"This is your day. Go have fun," Earl pointed outside.

Cal hugged his parents. "I love you guys! You're awesome!"

"I love you too, Son," Earl replied.

"Have a good time!" Cal's mom, Regina, called out.

Thirty-one flavors of ice cream covered the hills and lawns and streets of Chewandswallow. Kids all over town kept shouting, "Ice cream!"

Cal leaped headfirst into the snow and made a face-down snow angel. He played with his friends, then Earl took him on a sled ride off their snowy roof.

Flint watched as the two slid past and crashed happily into a Dumpster full of ice cream. He sighed, wishing that he could be sledding with his dad. That would be great. But no matter what Flint did, his father would never be proud of him.

Just then Sam came up to Flint. "Flint, this is amazing!" she said. "And designing the ice cream to accumulate into scoops? I don't know how you're gonna top this!"

"Maybe with hot fudge?" he said with a grin.

"Hey, Flint," Cal called. "You wanna be in a snowball fight with us?"

Flint suddenly felt very awkward and didn't have an answer for Cal.

"Flint, what's the problem?" Sam asked.

53

"I've never actually been in a snowball fight," he admitted.

"Really?" Sam asked, stunned.

Flint shrugged. "I don't even know the rules. Is there, like, a point system or is it to the death?"

Taking a deep breath, he scooped up some ice cream and tossed the ball weakly. "So, like this?"

"No. Harder than that," Sam said as she showed Flint how to pack a snowball.

Once Flint got it, there was no stopping him. "Snowball! Snowball! Snowball!" he chanted as he threw one after another.

Sam watched, happy for Flint as he enjoyed his very first snowball fight. "Well, there's something to be said for enthusiasm," she remarked.

"Sam!" Flint called out, running past her, with some kids hot on his heels. "I'm one of the guys now!" For the first time in his life, Flint felt like he belonged.

Sam instructed Manny to take wide shots of Flint and the children enjoying the ice cream. She spoke directly to the camera, knowing that this was a very special report. "I scream, you scream, we all scream for Flint Lockwood's latest tasty townwide treat, with flurries of frozen fun on what the mayor declared to be an ice-cream snow day."

Chapter 7

After her ice-cream snow day report, Sam sealed her place as a celebrity reporter.

People around the globe tuned in to see her weather reports from Chewandswallow. From New York to Paris to Cairo to London, everyone wanted to know what was on the menu in this small town.

The mayor was eagerly preparing for all the tourists he had invited to see Chewandswallow's wonders for themselves. A grand reopening celebration was planned for next Saturday, and the world was abuzz with excitement.

One afternoon, after Sam had finished her weather report for the day, Flint took her up a grassy hill, a short distance from the town center. What she didn't know was that he had programmed the machine to prepare a very special surprise—just for her.

"Where are we going?" Sam asked.

"Oh, nowhere, I just thought it'd be nice for the two of us to . . . ," he said, stalling, enjoying the suspense, "go on a walk together. Like you do . . . as friends."

Suddenly he feigned surprise—"Oh my, what's that?"—then grinned as Sam froze.

"Wow!" she exclaimed.

On the top of the hill was an enormous castle made out of yellowish orange Jell-O.

"Oh." Sam squealed in delight, clasping her hands together. "Jell-O's my favorite!"

"You never made a special request so I made one for you," Flint explained, beaming from ear to ear.

He stepped into the Jell-O mold. Sam looked confused for a second, unsure of where he had gone, but Flint called to her and pulled Sam inside.

"Whoa!" Sam said.

"Everything's made of Jell-O," Flint pointed out. "This piano, those sconces, that boom box, that aquarium, that *Venus de Milo* with your face on it next to a Michelangelo's *David* that also has your face."

Sam was speechless, torn between thinking Flint was wonderful and thinking he was weird, but absolutely in awe of her Jell-O surroundings.

"Come on, Sam, what are you waiting for?" Flint asked.

She paused for a second and then decided that weird was wonderful! Sam joined Flint in leaping up and down on the Jell-O, and threw in a few fast little manic jumps as well.

"Wooo! Yeahhhhh!" she shouted.

A while later, as the sun began to set, Sam and Flint rested in the dome at the top of the Jell-O creation.

"So, Jell-O," Sam said softly.

"Right, right, right," Flint sputtered nervously.

"It's a solid. It's a liquid. It's a viscoelastic polymer made of polypeptide chains, but you eat it–" Sam stopped, realizing that she sounded like a nerd. "I mean . . . it tastes good," she said with a giggle.

Flint drew his eyebrows together. "Why do you do that?" he asked.

"Do what?" Sam asked, staring out at the sunset.

"Say something smart and then bail from it?"

Sam turned to face him. "Can you keep a secret?"

"No," Flint replied honestly. "But this time, sure."

"Okay, well, it was a really long time ago, but I too was . . . a nerd," Sam nervously confessed.

"Too?" Flint asked uncomfortably.

Sam began to tell Flint about her childhood.

"When I was a little girl, I wore a ponytail, I had glasses, and I was totally obsessed with the science of weather. Other girls wanted a Barbie, I wanted a Doppler Weather Radar 2000 Turbo. But all the kids used to taunt me with this stupid song: 'Four eyes! Four eyes! You need glasses to see!'" Sam sighed. "It wasn't even clever."

Flint wanted to laugh at the song, but held back. "Go on," he said encouragingly.

"So I got a new look, gave up the sciency smart stuff, and I was never made fun of again. And I still need these glasses, but I never wear them." Sam pulled a pair of glasses from her pocket.

"I'll bet you look great with glasses on," Flint said.

"Oh, I'm really not–," Sam began to protest, but Flint grabbed her glasses and put them on her.

"And on they go," he insisted.

"Oh," Sam said as the blurry guy in front of her suddenly became crystal clear.

"Wait." Flint reached behind him and quickly carved something out of Jell-O. "It's a Jell-O scrunchie." He leaned over and pulled her hair back into a ponytail.

"Now, the reveal!" Flint leaned back to get a good look at the real Sam Sparks.

"Wow," he said. "I mean, you were okay before, but now you're . . . beautiful."

"No, I'm not." Sam blushed. "I can't go out in public like this."

"Well, why not?" Flint asked. "I mean, this is the real you, right? Smart, bespectacled . . . Who wouldn't want to see that?"

Sam was completely charmed. "You know, I've never met anyone like you, Flint Lockwood."

Just then Flint's cell phone announced that he had a call. Flint tried to ignore it, but Sam asked, "Is your phone ringing?"

Flint looked at the caller ID. "It's the mayor. Do you mind if I take this?"

"No, no, no," Sam said. "Go ahead and take it. That's fine, really. I should be going, anyway."

"I'm so sorry, I'm just going to step outside real quick," Flint told her, then into the phone he said, "Mr. Mayor?"

After listening for a second, his voice rose in surprise. "You have big news?"

That evening Tim was standing on a street corner under the dim light of the shadowed moon, waiting for Flint. He was wearing a suit and tie.

"Dad!" Flint called out, excited to tell him about the mayor's invitation. "Thank you for coming!"

Tim tugged at his tie uncomfortably. "Do I look all right?"

"You look great, come on!" Flint grabbed his father's hand and led him toward a fancy restaurant nearby. "We have so much to celebrate, Dad."

Inside the restaurant, Flint and Tim were escorted to the best table.

"Very nice place," Tim said, looking around. The restaurant had removed its roof and ceiling.

Flint was a major celebrity. Tourists were calling his name, and Joe Towne raised his glass as Flint walked by. "A toast! To Flint and his delicious steaks."

"Wasn't this the diner?" Tim asked as they sat down.

"Yeah, but it's way better," Flint said.

"So, no roof?" Tim stared up at the ominous-looking clouds overhead.

"Yup. You just hold out your plate. I even made it rain your favorite: meat." Flint pushed out his plate and caught a large steak.

Clank, clank, clank! Large steaks were landing on the tables around them, rattling silverware. Everyone seemed to be enjoying it, except for Tim. He was very wary about the whole food-falling-from-the-sky thing.

Flint was more concerned about telling his dad his big news. He took a deep breath and nervously began, "Okay, so you know how the grand reopening of the town is tomorrow? Well, the mayor has asked *me* to cut the ribbon. He said my invention saved the town! Aren't you proud of me?"

Slam! A large slab of meat fell onto Tim's plate, startling him. "Well," he said, "doesn't this steak look a little big to you?"

"Yeah, it's a big steak. Every steak is not exactly the same size." Flint was confused at his dad's reaction. "Did you even hear what I just said?"

Wham! Another large steak landed between them, knocking the glassware off their table.

"Son, look around. I'm not sure this is good for people. Maybe you should think about turning this thing off," Tim replied with a frown.

Flint glowered at his dad. "It's making everybody happy," he said, his voice tight. "Everybody except you. When are you going to accept that this is who I

61

am instead of trying to get me to work in some boring tackle shop?"

And just then Flint was hit in the head by a massive piece of steak.

"Well, you seem like you know what you're doing," Tim answered as he got up from the table. "I guess I'll just get out of your way."

This was not the way Flint had imagined his special evening with his dad would turn out. Not at all.

Chapter 8

Back at his shop, Tim was sad about the way things were with his son, but he knew that he was right. Something was terribly wrong with the weather machine. As if to prove his point, a giant hot dog fell from the sky and knocked off the AND SON part of the shop sign.

Across town, Flint was walking toward his lab, muttering to himself. "There's no pleasing that guy. He just wants to take anything good I do and just smoosh it—aaah!"

Flint screamed as a three-foot long hot dog suddenly crashed down in front of him.

Looking around, he saw that giant hot dogs had fallen all around the neighborhood. "These *are* big hot dogs," Flint noted. At that moment a bad feeling came over the inventor, and he hurried over to the lab.

On the scanner in his lab was an image of a huge hot dog. Flint glanced over at Steve, whose face was smeared with ketchup and mustard. "Oh, man. This isn't that bad, right, Steve?"

"Yellow," Steve said simply.

Flint went to the Dangeometer. "You're right, Steve. The Dangeometer is in the yellow." He ran his hands nervously through his hair. "I don't know what to do."

At that moment, a strange whirring sound caught Flint's attention. He turned around to see the mayor entering the lab in an electric wheelchair. The mayor was eating a hot dog piled with other kinds of food.

"I do . . . declare these hot dogs to be delicious!" the mayor said, taking a messy bite. Bits of food spilled from the corners of his mouth and dripped onto his very big belly.

Flint barely recognized the mayor. He was incredibly enormous. Flint understood why the mayor would need the wheelchair to get around.

"Big," Steve said, then ran away.

"How did you get in here?" Flint asked.

The mayor didn't answer Flint's question. Instead he said, "Tomorrow's the big day, Flint. The entire town's fate is resting on your food weather! I'm thinking pasta, some light appetizers. I know you won't let us down." He wheeled backward into the shadows.

"Mr. Mayor," Flint called after him. "I think there's something you should see."

The mayor returned. "What?" he asked, rolling back into view.

Flint pulled up a display on the computer monitor.

"This is the molecular structure of a hot dog that fell last week. And this is the molecular structure of a hot dog that fell today." Flint pushed a button revealing a very scary-looking, rapidly moving group of molecules. "The machine uses microwave radiation to mutate the genetic recipe of the food. The more we ask it to make, the more clouds it takes in, the more radiation it emits, the more these food molecules could overmutate. I think that's why the food is getting bigger."

The mayor laughed. "Here's what I heard: 'Blah blah blah science science science bigger.' And bigger *is* better. Everyone's going to love these new portion sizes. I know I do."

"My dad thinks I should turn it off. . . ."

"Geniuses like us are never understood by their fathers, Flint," the mayor said.

"But what if—?" Flint began, but was cut short.

"Who needs the approval of one family member when you can have it from millions of acquaintances, not to mention that cute little Sam Sparks . . . and me? I've always felt you were like a son to me, Flint. And I'm going to be so proud of you tomorrow when you cut that ribbon, save the town, and prove to everybody what a great inventor you are. So here's the cheese: You can keep it going, get everything you've ever wanted, and be the great man I know you can be. Or you can turn it off, ruin everything, and no one will ever like you. It's your choice."

There were a few minutes of silence as Flint thought about what the mayor said. "Okay," he finally said, although he didn't sound too sure. "I mean, bigger is better, right?"

"Oh, yeah," the mayor said, with just a hint of creepiness in his voice.

Flint pushed the button on the computer, sending the next day's menu to the FLDSMDFR.

In the morning, Sam was sitting in the weather van, getting ready to report on the grand reopening of Chewandswallow's tourist attractions. "It's very stormy outside," she mumbled to herself.

Sam couldn't decide what to wear for that day's report: glasses or no glasses. She put them on and took them off, then put them on again. When she had them on, it amazed Sam how clear the world became. She had grown used to things being completely fuzzy all the time.

With her perfect vision, Sam noticed a small, old-fashioned case tucked in the corner of the van. A note on top of the case read: DOPPLER RADAR 2000 TURBO. Sam grabbed the case, opened it, and pushed the start button. The Doppler machine booted up. Sam adjusted some knobs and . . . *beep, beep, beep.* A red spinning glow crossed the weather screen. Sam knew exactly what that red glow meant. It wasn't good.

A second later, a flash of lightning blazed across the sky. Sam ran outside. She *had* to warn Flint.

A dozen cruise ships were parked in the harbor, and thousands of happy tourists wandered through town while thousands more filled the city square. Oversize appetizers rained down from the sky.

The mayor stood on a stage. "Hey, hey, hey!" he called out. "Welcome, tourists, to Chewandswallow!" He crossed in front of the biggest ribbon anyone had ever seen. The crowd cheered.

"That is one big mayor," a tourist remarked as the mayor continued his speech.

"Delight in our Nacho Cheese Hotsprings! Allow your kids to eat all the junk food they want in our completely unsupervised Kidz Zone! And when the fun is done, graze upon the sunset cresting over Mount Leftovers, from which we're protected by a presumably indestructible dam. We've got people here today from all around the world, from as far as China to West Virginia."

Backstage, Flint was anxiously awaiting his introduction. He was disappointed to see that the seat reserved for his dad was empty.

Sam rushed up to him. "You need to look at this," she said, pointing to the image on the Doppler 2000.

"Why aren't you on TV?" Flint asked, a little annoyed. "You're supposed to be broadcasting this."

"There's a problem," Sam replied. " I think the food's getting bigger–"

"I know, it's great. Bigger portion sizes. Everyone loves it," Flint said as he pointed at a tourist catching a jumbo jumbo prawn in his hat.

Sam tried to make herself clear. "Flint, I'm not sure we're doing the right thing here."

"Sam, listen–," Flint began, but was interrupted.

"What if we've bit off more than we can chew?" Sam asked.

Flint snorted. "For the first time in my life, everybody loves something that I've done. Why can't you just be happy for me and go say the weather!"

Sam could not believe it as Flint turned away from her and gave his full attention to the mayor's glowing introduction.

"And now, without further ado, our town's hero and my metaphorical son, Flint Lockwood!"

Leaving Sam to stare after him in disgust, Flint ran onstage to thunderous applause. He soaked it all in. "Thank you! Thank you, everyone! Yeah! Woo!"

The mayor turned to Brent. "Will you please hand over the ceremonial scissors?"

"But—" Brent was shocked. Cutting the ribbon had always been his job. And he definitely wasn't going to allow that loser Flint Lockwood to take this away from him.

The mayor had to wrestle the scissors away from Brent, who started crying, "No! You can't! You can't take them! I'm Baby Brent! Uh-oh!" And then he whipped off his tracksuit to reveal his ever-present diaper.

For the first time in Brent's life, the crowd booed

69

him! "Put your clothes back on!" someone hollered.

Brent fled the stage in tears. He could not believe that he was no longer the hero of the town.

The mayor handed the ceremonial scissors to Flint. The crowd began chanting, "Lockwood! Lockwood!"

"Go ahead, Flint," the mayor told him. "Everyone loves you."

Flint raised the scissors as everyone hollered and cheered. With a dramatic flourish, Flint cut the ribbon, and Chewandswallow was officially open to tourists. People rushed through the town. They played in the park, shopped in the local stores, and swam in the hot springs.

Things seemed to be going well until a flock of Ratbirds flew overhead. And then Steve started running and shouting, "Danger! Danger! Danger!"

Flint called after him, "Steve!" but his voice was lost in a gust of wind.

"Achoo!" Flint sneezed.

Sam also sneezed. Everyone in town began to sneeze.

Flint tasted the air. "Salt-and-pepper wind?" he remarked, before he was hit in the head by a giant leaf. "Oregano," he said. Then he looked across the town—right at a massive spaghetti twister that was ten blocks away, but moving fast in their direction.

"Mamma mia!" Flint exclaimed. Sam had warned him, but Flint hadn't listened. And now it might be too late. Sam gave Flint a nasty glare, then ran off toward her van.

"Sam, wait, no! I can turn it off!" he called after her. Angry, she ignored him.

Flint looked up at the twister. "I *can* turn it off," he repeated to himself, hoping it was true. Determined now to shut down his machine, Flint ran toward his lab as the twister wound its way around the town, and huge meatballs crashed all around.

People were running toward the docks, in the direction opposite to where Flint needed to go. He was like a salmon swimming upstream. A telephone pole flew by, but Flint pressed on. The winds were so strong that he was literally running on air. A man in a bathtub soared past.

Flint was close to home now, but the winds were getting even stronger. He was almost swept away. "No!" Flint screamed as his precious lab coat blew off.

Fighting his way through the swirling spaghetti noodles, Flint finally reached the Port-a-Potty door, where Steve was waiting for him.

"Gummi bears," Steve said in way of greeting.

"Not now, Steve." Flint snatched the monkey up onto his shoulder, and the two of them took the elevator to the lab.

The spaghetti twister caused all kinds of trouble throughout Chewandswallow.

The cruise ships gathered up their tourists and backed out of town as fast as they could. Everyone was running for cover to avoid being buried by spaghetti and meatballs.

Police Officer Earl was out in the storm, looking for his son. "Cal! Cal! Where's my son?" he called out as spaghetti sauce splashed on him.

Earl ran past Sam, who was giving her weather report from Sardine Circle. Sam was wearing her glasses with her hair tied back in the Jell-O scrunchie ponytail.

"This is Sam Sparks, live from Chewandswallow, where a spaghetti twister—"

The WNN anchor in New York cut her off. "Whoa, whoa, Sam, hey! We love a good storm over here, but you look like a nerd."

Sam ignored him and stuck to her report. "Patrick, several children are stranded in the path of this tomato tornado."

Manny panned the camera over to the Kidz Zone.

There, Cal and the other kids had finally stopped gorging themselves. They tried to run from the tornado, but after eating so much junk food, the kids were slow and tired.

"My tummy hurts," Cal moaned lamely into Manny's camera.

Through the window of a TV repair shop, Earl saw his son on a TV. "Cal!" he shouted, then rushed toward the Kidz Zone.

Cal was sprawled on the ground, directly in the path of the tornado when Earl spotted him. "Hold on, Son! I'm coming! Cal!" But even athletic Earl wasn't fast enough. He watched in terror as his son was swept into the noodle twister.

Sam continued her live report. "It's becoming a tomato tornado nightmare—"

The network anchor interrupted her again. "Yikes. What is that, a scrunchie? I haven't seen one of those since 1995!"

Sam was furious. This wasn't the time to talk about hair and glasses! "We have an actual weather emergency!" she yelled, just as she got smashed by a glob of spaghetti.

Kshhh. The news feed went out.

"We'll get right back to that storm," the WNN

anchor said, laughing so hard that he was near tears. "And hopefully Sam will look a little more appealing." He clearly had no clue what the storm in Chewandswallow meant, and the station cut over to report on other, less interesting, weather patterns around the country.

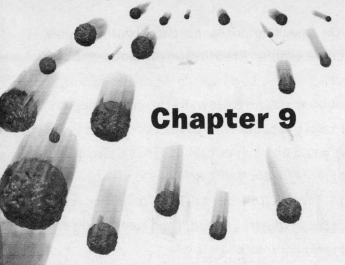

Chapter 9

"Steve, we just have to upload the kill code and it will shut down the–" Flint had just burst into his lab, only to discover the mayor sitting at his computer terminal.

"Oaaaaah!" Flint shouted. "No! What are you doing?"

The mayor was typing on Flint's keyboard. "I've been ordering up dinner for the last ten minutes. Why? Is something going on?"

"I've got to stop the machine," Flint told the mayor. "There's a spaghetti twister tearing up the town!"

Flint rushed toward the computer, but was stopped by the mayor's massive belly.

"Oh, it can't be that bad," the mayor said calmly as he pressed the big red send button on the console. On the computer screen, food images began to circle around, creating an ominous strobe-light effect.

Flint got up and started toward the console again. "I can still stop the order with the kill code!"

"I knew you'd chicken out, Flint. That's why I had to keep the gravy train going so I could still bring in the *bread*." The mayor clocked Flint over the head with a huge piece of garlic bread, then rushed toward him wielding an enormous carrot.

Flint charged back, using an oversize asparagus to shove the man away. He made it to his computer. "Sending kill code," he said as he pressed a series of keys and was nearly done when the mayor lunged at him.

"Don't be so *shellfish*," the mayor said as he hooked Flint in the curve of a jumbo jumbo prawn.

"Food fight! Food fight!" Steve cheered.

Flint refused to give up. He grabbed a huge hot pepper and shoved it in the mayor's eye. "Aahh!" the mayor cried out.

Flint headed back to the computer, but the mayor was ready with another weapon. "Sorry, Flint, it's *nacho* day!"

The mayor threw a handful of oversize nacho

chips at Flint, like ninja stars, which pinned him to the ground.

"Well, Flint, it's been a pleasure to *beet* you!" The mayor grabbed a gigantic beet and threw it at Flint.

After struggling for a bit, Flint managed to break free from the chips and dodged the soaring vegetable in the nick of time. Unfortunately the beet hit the FLDSMDFR's satellite dish, smashing it into pieces.

Hopeful that he could still stop the machine, Flint used his last burst of energy to send the kill code.

But he was too late. A warning flashed on the screen: ERROR: CONNECTION LOST.

Flint was stunned and horrified. "That was the only way to communicate with the machine," he gravely told to the mayor. "What exactly did you order?"

"A Vegas-style all-you-can-eat buffet," the mayor replied.

While the two stared at the computer monitor in Chewandswallow, up in space, the FLDSMDFR glowed an ominous red. "Food walla," the machine voiced, and then it kicked into overdrive.

Outside, it appeared as though the worst was over. The clouds parted, revealing a clear, light blue sky.

The twister was gone, but its destructive force could be seen all over town. People slowly emerged from the rubble, still in disbelief at what had just happened.

Sam dusted herself off, and was relieved to see that Manny had also survived the twister. She quickly opened up her Doppler 2000 to monitor the weather.

Just then Earl came running up, with Cal in his arms. "Help, somebody! Help me, please! It's my son. He's not moving."

"We need a doctor!" Sam shouted. "Is anyone here a doctor? Anyone?"

"I am a doctor," Manny said calmly, setting down his camera.

"You are?" Sam asked, surprised.

"I was, back in Guatemala. I came here for a better life. Pretty great decision, eh?" Manny reached into his pocket and pulled out a stethoscope. He listened carefully to Cal's heart.

"How is he, Doc?" Earl asked as a small crowd gathered around.

"He's in a food coma," Manny answered. "Too much junk food. I need celery, stat!"

Joe Towne handed over a stalk of celery. "Here you go."

Manny snapped it in half and waved it under Cal's nose.

Instantly Cal coughed and woke up. "Daddy?" he called weakly.

"Oh, Cal . . . Cal! I love you, Son." Earl was so happy, he didn't care when Cal puked all over his shoes and uniform. "Thank goodness everything is all right."

"No, it's not okay," Sam announced. "That spaghetti twister was small potatoes compared to what's on the way." She handed Manny his camera. "Manny, patch us through. Go!"

Sam interrupted the reporter on WNN, breaking in with emergency news.

"Hey!" The New York anchor looked at Sam on the monitor. "Four eyes?"

"Can it, Patrick!" she scolded. "We are about to be in the epicenter of a perfect food storm. It's going to spread across the globe. I've calculated the Coriolis acceleration of the storm system. First it'll hit New York, then Paris, then the Jiayuguan Pass in eastern China. And in four hours, the entire Northern Hemisphere will be one big potluck."

Tim came out of his shop to survey the disaster. He stepped on something soft.

When he picked up the thing, he realized it was Flint's lab coat, covered in mud and pasta sauce. He tucked the coat under his arm and hurried off to find his son.

As he passed by a junkyard, Tim heard a low moan. Concerned that someone was hurt, he followed the sound—and found Flint, curled up in a rusty barrel and staring at his can of Spray-On Shoes.

"Flint?" Tim called gently.

"Hey, Dad," Flint replied.

"What are you doing?"

"Well, I tried to help everybody, but instead I ruined everything. I'm just a piece of junk, so I threw myself away, along with all these dumb inventions." Flint held up a bag full of everything he had ever invented. "This is all junk."

Tim wasn't comfortable dealing with feelings, but he tried to comfort Flint. "Well, Son, you . . . listen, when your boat is . . . when it's listing, if it's not running . . . you know, uh–"

"Don't worry, I get it," Flint said. "Mom was wrong

about me. I'm not an inventor. I should've just quit when you said." Flint took one last look at the can of Spray-On Shoes, then threw it away. "This is junk."

Tim set Flint's dirty lab coat over the rim of the barrel. "Well, when it rains, you put on a coat," he advised.

Flint sighed. "Dad, you know I don't understand fishing meta–" Flint looked up and spotted the lab coat. "What?"

Suddenly, for the first time, Flint had use for one of Tim's fishing metaphors. Flint was going to thank his dad, but Tim had left.

Flint jumped out of the barrel, put on his lab coat, and grabbed his bag of old inventions. He knew *exactly* what he needed to do!

Flint called for his trusty assistant. "Come on, Steve. We've got *diem* to *carpe*."

Working quickly, Flint went to the lab and downloaded the kill code onto a USB flash drive. "Kill code downloading. Redesigning. Virtualizing. Cutting. Welding. Forging. Wiring."

"Helping," said the monkey.

"Testing," Flint said. Then, "Yes!"

What Flint needed at this moment was his car. After the first Flying Car was electrocuted, Flint built another model, and it was now about to help him save the world.

With a quick turn of the key, the engine fired up and the lights went on. A flick of his wrist made the wings pop open.

Flint was on his way.

Chapter 10

Across Chewandswallow, chaos reigned as the Vegas-style buffet rained down. An enormous jelly bean flipped over a car. Gigantic hams pierced the roof of the cannery. Sam dove out of the way of a massive fried egg, just before it flattened a truck nearby. Mammoth chocolate doughnuts rolled down the street after Brent. A man flailed his arms, trying futilely to get a huge macaroni off his head.

Slap! A gargantuan pancake covered the school. "No school!" the kids shouted with joy.

Screech! Driving fast and furious, Flint skidded his car into the center of Sardine Circle. He quickly parked, then rushed up to Sam. But she turned her back to him, arms crossed.

He knew Sam was listening, even if she wasn't

looking at him, so he took a deep breath and said, "Everyone! I want to apologize." Then in a gentler voice, he said, "Especially to you, Sam."

He turned back to the crowd, and spoke confidently, "I was a selfish jerk, and I put the entire world at risk. But I have a plan. This flash drive contains a kill code. I will fly up into that food storm, plug it into the machine, and shut it down forever. The rest of you will evacuate the island on boats made of toast and Swiss cheese. What do you say, gang?"

Flint expected the town to rally behind him. Instead, the mayor shouted, "This is all his fault! Get him!"

And the crowd agreed! "Yeah! Get Flint! Let's rock his car back and forth!"

Under attack, Flint jumped back into his car. Steve locked the doors.

"Hey!" Everyone turned as Earl strode up to Flint's car-plane and jumped onto the hood. "This mess we're in, it's all our fault." The crowd grew quiet. "Me, it was my job to protect and serve the people, and I didn't even protect my own son." Earl sighed.

Sam thought about what Earl was saying. He was right. Brent also agreed with the cop.

"Look," Earl went on. "I'm as mad at Flint as you are. In fact, when he gets out of that car, I'm going to slap him in the face." At that, Flint flinched, but Earl wasn't done. "I know Flint Lockwood made the food, but it was made to order. And now it's time for all of us to pay the bill."

The crowd began to applaud.

"Thank you, Earl," Flint said, nervously getting out of the car and stepping up next to the man who had come to his defense.

Just like he said he would, Earl slapped Flint.

"Ow!" Flint cried out, pressing a hand to his cheek.

"Sorry," Earl apologized.

"It's okay." Flint shook hands with the cop.

Earl turned to the citizens of Chewandswallow. "Let's go build some boats!" he declared. He then led the cheering crowd over to the docks.

Sam climbed up onto the hood of Flint's car. "I'm coming with you," she told him. "You're gonna need someone to navigate you through that storm. I just can't let you do this alone."

Manny stepped onto the car to join them. "You are going to need a copilot."

"You're a pilot, too?" Sam asked in surprise.

"Yes," Manny told her. "I'm also a particle physicist."

"Really?" Sam was amazed.

Manny laughed. "No, that was a joke. I am also a comedian."

"I'm coming too!" Brent climbed up onto the car hood.

"Brent! Uh, that's okay." Flint brushed him away.

"No, it's not okay. I've been coasting on my fame since I was a baby, but it was all just an illusion. Maybe up there, I'll find out who I really am."

Flint considered the seating arrangements in his small car. "Uh, car's pretty full, and we don't really—"

Without waiting for Flint to say no again, Brent squeezed into the backseat with the monkey.

The team was ready so Flint set the car-plane in motion. Up and up they flew, past a flock of Ratbirds. Just before they reached the clouds, Flint took one final look at Chewandswallow. He could see his dad, standing outside the bait shop, boarding up the windows, preparing for more bad food weather.

Flint sighed as he watched his dad. He had really wanted to make his dad proud, and this was his last chance. What he couldn't hear was his dad, way down below, saying, "Good luck, Son."

86

Flint steered through the clouds, and the car-plane shook like crazy. A strange noise began beeping from under the passenger seat. Sam pulled out her Doppler and popped the lid. "Pea soup fog!" Sam announced just as a warm green mist covered the windshield.

Flint used the windshield wipers, but he still couldn't see a thing.

Bang! Something hit them. Sam took a long, hard look at the Doppler. "Flint, there's massive gastroprecipitation accumulated around the machine. It's almost as if it's—"

Flint realized what Sam was seeing and finished her thought, "—inside a giant meatball."

When the car-plane emerged from the soupy fog, they all clearly saw the problem. The machine was now deep inside a huge food asteroid a mile wide, with large globs of congealed leftover food adhered to the outside of the machine. They watched as rain clouds were sucked in through the top and then converted to enormous food, which then blasted out the bottom, toward Chewandswallow.

Flint was checking a readout when, all of a sudden, the car-plane rattled violently. An alarm went off. "What was that?" Flint asked, frantically looking around for the source.

"Anybody order pizza?" Sam asked as calmly as she could manage.

In the rearview mirror, Flint spotted a whole bunch of pizza slices following the car.

Brent couldn't believe what he was seeing. "The pizza is chasing us?"

"Sentient food?" Flint said. "That's impossible!"

"Unless its molecular structure's mutated into superfood–," Sam noted.

"–that's been genetically engineered to protect the FLDSMDFR," Flint finished.

The pizza slices attacked, and Flint zigged and zagged through the skies to narrowly avoid being hit. "Whew! That was close! I mean, can you imagine what would happen if we lost this kill code?" He held up the flash drive for everyone to see.

Suddenly–*flong!*–a mushroom slice broke through the car window. It knocked the flash drive out of Flint's hand–and sent it falling through the clouds.

"Uh-oh!" Brent said, and this time he wasn't trying to act.

Chapter 11

Tim watched the storm rage outside his bait shop. A giant ham hit the store windows, but the tape he'd put on the glass held strong and the ham bounced away.

Ring, ring! The desk phone blared. Tim reached over and answered, "Tim's Tackle Shop."

It was Flint, calling from above. "Dad, you're okay, great! Um, I need a favor. The fate of the world depends on it."

"Okay, Skipper, what do you need?" Tim asked.

"I just need you to go into my lab and get on my computer to e-mail a file to my cell phone."

Tim froze. He had never warmed up to computers, and the thought of having to use one made his palms sweat.

"Uhhh . . . who's going to man the shop?" Tim asked, stalling.

"There's no one in the shop," Flint replied.

Tim looked around the empty store and sighed. "All right," he said, before hanging up.

Up above, the pizza was now shooting toppings like missiles. Flint wasn't a good driver. In truth, he was awful. When Manny offered to take the wheel, Flint readily agreed. And it turned out that Manny was an incredible pilot. He easily dodged the pizza. Now they had a fighting chance!

Flint turned to study the Doppler, then announced, "Okay, here's the plan. Sam and I will enter the 'meateroid' through the intake here, which should lead us straight to the FLDSMDFR. Manny, you and Steve will stay on the plane."

Flint noticed Steve playing with his can of Spray-On Shoes and grabbed it, before adding, "Once my dad e-mails the kill code, we'll rendezvous here at the eastern blowhole in . . ."

He turned to Sam. "How long until the world is destroyed?" he asked calmly.

"Twenty minutes," she replied.

Seeing that everyone had a task, Brent felt left out. "What about me, Flint, what do I do?"

Flint thought for a second, then answered. "Uh, you can be president of the backseat."

"Oh," Brent said, disappointed.

"Deploy hatch!" Flint instructed, and the hatch in the car's roof popped off as on a fighter jet. "Seat belts off." He and Sam unbuckled. "Barrel roll!" Manny flipped the car-plane over, dropping Sam and Flint through the roof. Flint went out first, followed by Sam, who held on to her Doppler.

Just then Brent jumped out after them. "Wait for me!" he yelled.

"As long as we stay on course, it should be a straight shot to the–," Sam had started to say before Brent slammed into her. She then bumped into Flint, throwing them all off course.

Flint, Sam, and Brent screamed as they tumbled through the dark tunnel. After a few minutes of free fall, the three crash-landed onto an unfamiliar surface. Fumbling around, Flint created a torch from a marshmallow and a shrimp skewer. Suddenly they could see that the walls of the tunnel were made entirely of congealed food.

"Where are we?" Brent asked, plugging his nose

from the overwhelming number of mixed-up scents.

"I don't know, but I think I lost my appetite," Flint answered as he looked around.

Sam used the Doppler as a guide. "We've landed here in some kind of exhaust vent. But if we go this way, the FLDSMDFR should be right down this air shaft," she said, pointing down a small but deep tunnel.

The three of them began to crawl in the direction Sam indicated. At the end of the tunnel they faced a huge cavern. Here they could stand, but there was a river of hot oil running down the center.

Brent took one look at the oil and said, "We're fried."

Determined not to give up, Flint and Sam rigged rafts from bits of food that they found. Halfway across the hot, oily river, Flint's phone began to ring.

Flint eagerly answered, "Dad! Okay, on the screen there's a file marked 'Kill Code.'"

"Wha–?" Tim replied.

Knowing his father's fear of computers, Flint gave him instructions that he thought were simple enough for Tim to follow. "Move that into my e-mail window, type in my name, and press send," Flint said.

"Right," Tim said at first, then, "What?" He was baffled.

Flint was floating down the hot oil river, trying desperately not to fry his feet. "You see the thing that looks like a little piece of paper?"

"Yeah," Tim said. Flint told him to use the mouse to drag it across the desktop, so Tim literally dragged the mouse across Flint's desk, and the keyboard went along with it.

Crash! Papers and equipment fell to the floor. "That didn't do anything," Tim reported.

"Aaaargh!" was all Flint managed to say.

Meanwhile the people of Chewandswallow had gathered near the pancake-covered school. They were busy building boats from pieces of gigantic bread, with Earl leading the charge.

"Hoist those sails," he commanded. "Toast that bread. We're running out of time." A rumbling noise made Earl look up. The dam above the city was quivering.

"Let's move out," Earl ordered. "Go, go, go! We can do it! Come on, move it, move it! Good job! That's what I'm talking about! Go, go."

When the bread boats were ready, Earl led the way to the docks—just as enormous hamburgers started to fall.

Then, at the exact moment the first boat was set into the water, the mayor showed up, pushing his way through the crowd. "Wait, wait," he said. "I have an important announcement."

Everyone made way for him and eagerly waited to hear him speak. But the mayor simply jumped into the first boat. "It's mayor time! See ya later," he said, laughing as he shoved off the docks. "It's a boat and a sandwich!"

The people stared at the departing mayor with disbelief, too shocked to speak. But then they heard a loud moan in the distance. It came from the dam that held back all the leftovers, now straining under the weight of the gigantic pile of food.

Cal sneaked away from his father to get a better look at the dam.

"Cal! What are you looking at?" Earl asked his son. Cal's eyes were transfixed on a small cherry that had just landed on top of the dam.

All of a sudden the dam burst, creating an avalanche of food! Everyone started tossing their boats into the water and rushing to get as far away from the huge wave of food that was rolling toward them.

Cal was still staring at the avalanche when Earl snatched him up. Together with Regina, Earl and Cal were the last ones to cast off—just in the nick of time.

"Everybody head south!" Earl shouted. "We've got to stay ahead of that storm!"

Across town, in Flint's lab, Tim was trying for the second time to upload the kill code.
"Now what?" Tim asked.

"Just click send!" Flint yelled. "Dad, hurry!"

"Send? Send?" Tim asked, feeling the pressure of his task. "Oh, wait." Tim finally found the send button, and was about to send the file when a huge banana crashed through the lab!

Tim was struck down, and the lab phone hit the floor.

"Dad? Dad? Can you hear me?" Flint called out, feeling utterly helpless.

Flint stared at his cell phone. There was no Plan B. He had absolutely no idea what to do next.

Just then an odd noise startled him back into focus. *"Chk, chk, chk, chk."* It sounded like a chicken clucking—but that was impossible, wasn't it?

"Hey, guys?" Brent said, his voice cracking with nerves.

Sam and Flint looked up to see giant roasted chickens hovering over them. This was not good. Flint, Sam, and Brent began to run, but it was no use. The chickens dropped down and blocked their escape.

The chicken leader inched closer to Brent, with a hungry look in its eyes. For some strange reason, Brent suddenly didn't feel scared. "Aww, I don't know, I think they're kinda cute," he said. "I mean, this one just walked right up to me and–"

The chicken opened wide and swallowed Brent, mid-sentence, right down its gullet.

"They ate Breeeennnt!" Sam shrieked, before collapsing against Flint.

The remaining chickens completely surrounded Flint and Sam.

Flint put his phone to his ear, not certain if there was any way his father could hear him. "Dad, I'm surrounded by man-eating chickens right now, and if this is good-bye, I just want you to know . . . you're a great dad."

Flint then turned back to the chicken leader. He looked directly into its eyes–and begged, "Please don't eat me!"

Chapter 12

The sound of Flint's voice brought a spark of life back to Tim. Using every last bit of energy that he had, he raised his arm toward the keyboard—and pressed the send button.

The next second the lab was crushed by the food avalanche.

After gobbling up Brent, the chicken leader was still hungry, and it seemed that Flint and Sam were next on the menu. The giant bird moved in for the swallow when Flint's phone began to sound off. "Flint, you've got some mail. Flint, you've got some mail." The phone repeated the message again and again.

The noise confused the chicken just long enough

for Flint to flip open the phone. The message read:
E-MAIL RECEIVED. SUBJECT KILL CODE.

"Dad!" Flint exclaimed, with hope in his voice.

But the hungry chicken swiped the phone out of his hand. Flint lunged forward to get it back, and the bird suddenly keeled over.

Just then Brent shoved his head through the neck of the chicken and shouted, "Rahhh!" He also poked his arms and legs out of the chicken's body.

"Baby Brent?" Flint and Sam said at the same time.

"I'm not Baby Brent. I'm Chicken Brent, and I'm finally contributing to society," Brent declared. He then went to battle, punching and kicking the other chickens in a chicken fight.

Chicken Brent managed to hold off the angry chickens for a minute while he snatched up Sam and Flint. Placing them in a safer area, he told them, "Now go, you crazy kids, and save the world."

"You did it, Chicken Brent!" Flint shouted. "You really did it!"

Flint and Sam quickly escaped, leaving Brent to finish his battle. They were guided by Sam's Doppler, and they made their way to the FLDSMDFR.

"It should be right down this hole," Sam said,

pointing at a nasty-looking pit lined with stalactites.

Sam took a closer look at the stalactites. "That's peanut brittle," she reported. "If either one of us touches it, we'll go into anaphylactic shock."

Flint decided that it was time to tell the truth. "You know, actually, I'm not entirely allergic to peanuts. I might have just said that to get you to like me."

Sam snorted. "You really are bad with girls."

Down below, the townspeople of Chewandswallow were frantically sailing their bread boats in the ocean. They were struggling to stay afloat amid falling alphabet soup letters.

The mayor, however, seemed happy enough, eating his boat as he drifted along. "Well, one more nibble won't hurt," he kept saying as he bit off more of his boat.

The food problems weren't just in Chewandswallow anymore. Across the globe, food was falling, massive food that was causing massive destruction.

In New York City, a cab driver was plowed down by a sesame bagel, and a kosher pickle sent other cabs flying. In Paris, a club sandwich used the Eiffel Tower as a toothpick, and then an olive landed on its top. At Mount Rushmore, black clouds rolled in, then four cream pies hit the rocky faces of the presidents. Stonehenge was knocked over by ice cream sandwiches. Corn rolled over the Great Wall of China. Hot tea rained down on Big Ben in London.

At WNN, the studio finally realized that the destructive weather system was newsworthy. The anchor announced, "It looks like the food storm is following an unusual pattern of hitting the world's most famous landmarks first, and is now spreading to the rest of the—Oh my!"

A huge pretzel suddenly crashed through the TV station, and the broadcast was over.

All over the world the overloaded FLDSMDFR caused destruction, chaos, and tremendous stomach-aches. But there was hope. High above the Earth, Flint and his gang were working desperately to shut down the machine—forever.

Brent continued to hold off the chickens while Sam lowered Flint down the hole, using a licorice rope.

"After I plug my phone into the FLDSMDFR and destroy it, I'll tug on the licorice twice and you'll pull me back up," Flint told her.

"Sounds great," she said.

At that moment steam shot up the hole toward Sam. The licorice got wet and sticky, and Sam struggled to hold on to the slippery rope. Suddenly she lost her grip, and Flint began to fall.

Sam scrambled to catch the rope, and slipped down the tunnel, catching it but also catching a shard of peanut brittle on her arm. "Oh, no!" she said with a gasp.

Flint knew immediately what had happened. "You got cut, didn't you?" he called up from the hole.

Sam was having trouble breathing, but she didn't want Flint to worry. "It's just a scratch," she lied.

Flint wasn't going to let her risk her life. "Brent!" he shouted. "You need to take Sam back to the plane before she goes into shock!"

Brent agreed, even though he was barely holding off the marauding chickens. But Sam did not want to leave Flint alone.

"Let go, Sam," Flint said. "If you stay here, you will die."

"But if I leave you, *you'll* die," Sam replied. "Flint, you'll be stuck down there."

Flint looked down into the pit. "It's not ideal, no," he admitted.

"Come with us," Sam insisted. "We'll start over. We'll live underground. Use bacon for clothes."

"Sam, that's not a very good plan," Flint told her.

"It is, if it means I don't have to lose you!" Sam said, struggling to say what she was really feeling. "Look, I like you, okay?"

"*Like* me? Like, as a friend?" asked Flint, delighted to hear how Sam felt about him.

"No, like . . . *like* you . . . like you," she admitted.

"Me too," Flint said with a smile. "But about you."

He bit through the licorice rope and tumbled backward into the darkness. "Good-bye, Sam," he said.

Sam screamed, "Flint, no!" She tried to stand up, but, weakened by the peanut allergy, she stumbled backward.

Just then Chicken Brent rushed in, tossed her over his shoulder, and forcefully shoved aside giant roast chickens in his race to get out of the tunnel, to the car-plane.

Meanwhile Flint had landed on a strangely bumpy surface. It was an enormous food cavern. In the center of the room was the FLDSMDFR, encased in a column of gelatin and suspended above an undulating, bottomless pit. Flint cautiously made his way toward the machine, trying to be as quiet as possible.

Just as he got up close, he stepped on a crisp tortilla chip. *Crunch!* Immediately the top of the machine lifted up and, with military precision, fired giant corn niblets toward Flint.

"Corn," the machine's voice boomed in the cavern.

Flint managed to dive away before the corn hit him, which was lucky, because the corn made a huge crater when it struck the ground where Flint had just been standing.

Knowing that an intruder was around, the machine wasn't about to give up. It cast a beam of light across the floor, searching for its target. The beam passed over a row of food embedded in one of the walls. There were strawberries, hot dogs, bananas, and pickles.... But one hot dog wasn't really a hot dog. It was Flint.

Luckily the machine didn't see him and returned to work. Flint watched as the machine rhythmically inhaled, taking in clouds, then exhaled, dumping them out as food. Inhale, exhale, inhale, exhale.

Suddenly Flint had an idea. He quietly squeezed out of the hot dog bun and began climbing up the wall, using stuck-on food as stepping-stones. At the top he tied a long strand of spaghetti to a shrimp and, with a strong arm, tossed the hook across the cave. The tail of the shrimp wrapped itself around a doughnut hanging from the ceiling. Flint pulled the spaghetti strand to make certain it was secure and then–

The next time the machine exhaled, Flint let himself fly!

He swung on his spaghetti rope toward the machine and tied the end of the noodle around the tube where the food was sucked in. Then Flint opened his phone and prepared to deliver the kill code.

"I'm sorry, old friend," Flint said as he jammed the phone into the machine's port. But nothing happened.

"What the–?" Flint started to say, then realized that Tim had sent the cat DJ video instead of the kill code, and he couldn't help but laugh. His dad had tried to help, and that meant the world to Flint.

A second later the machine went out of control and began shooting food all over. Flint was tossed around. He held on tight, like a cowboy on a bucking bronco, as the FLDSMDFR tried to shake him off. The machine began pelting more food at Flint.

Somehow, through it all, the long noodle continued holding the shrimp, which held on to the doughnut, which held Flint, until–*snap!* Flint lost his balance and slipped, barely holding on as he dangled above the top of the machine. It opened and closed beneath him, chomping like a mouth.

Flint was slipping. . . .

In a nearby tunnel, Chicken Brent galloped along, with Sam on his back. The two were being chased by the flock of roasted chickens.

"Manny, we're on our way," Sam called into the two-way radio. Good thing Manny wasn't just a pilot, but a doctor as well, because Sam knew she was in trouble. "Hurry," she muttered, before fainting.

"Don't worry, I'm right outside," Manny reassured. "Everything is okeydokey."

Deftly, Manny brought the car up to collect his passengers when–

Thunk! Something hit the underside of the car wings.

"Vas is das?" Manny wondered aloud.

Alarmed by the jolt, Steve jumped onto Manny's face. "Scared," the monkey said.

Outside the car, a chunky paw reached up onto the wing. Steve and Manny looked over the side.

"Gummi bears!" Steve exclaimed. "Hungry, hungry gummi bears."

Delighted to have found his favorite food, Steve ate each bear that climbed onto the car. After a fierce and delicious battle, the bears were gone, but the car-plane was now spinning out of control.

When Brent and Sam reached the end of the tunnel, Brent was shocked to see the car-plane falling, a ruined wreck. He paused, not sure what to do.

"Oh, Manny, where are you?" Brent moaned.

The chicken army was coming up fast behind them, and Brent was left with two choices: jump and hope to land safely or be captured and get gobbled up.

He chose to jump.

Brent closed his eyes and leaped out of the blowhole into the air. The chickens followed, weakly flapping their roasted wings, and falling heavily. Brent held tight to Sam, wishing that there was some way–

Slam! Brent suddenly landed on something hard. It was the windshield of the car-plane! "Woo hoo!" Brent shouted with relief.

He carefully lowered Sam into the plane. "She touched a peanut or something," he told Manny.

While the doctor-pilot-comedian-cameraman was taking care of Sam, Flint was still barely hanging on to the spaghetti strand. His feet dangled above the FLDSMDFR pit as the machine continued to suck in clouds and convert them into weapons to fire at Flint.

He stared down into the gnashing teeth of the food hole, trying to think of a plan, when all of a sudden his feet gave him an idea. Flint was, of course, still wearing his permanent, indestructible Spray-On Shoes—and he realized how he could finally stop the machine.

"When it rains you put on a coat . . . of Spray-On Shoes!" Flint yelled. "Yes!"

He pulled out the can and sprayed a thick coating of shoe onto the chow plopper, sealing it shut.

The FLDSMDFR was no longer shooting food, but it now had all those clouds inside, and the blowhole was closed. Flint watched the food spout swell bigger and bigger until the giant balloon sac started to burst at the seams. Food was slowly trickling out. It was only a matter of time before the FLDSMDFR would explode.

Flint knew he had to get out at once, and there was only one way out. Closing his eyes tight, he let go of the noodle and dropped down through the food hole. Black smoke started to close in around him.

KA-BOOM!

The exploding food was forced out the same hole—and caught up with Flint.

"No!" Sam screamed as the food asteroid

exploded. Manny was flying the car-plane at top speed.

Chicken Brent tried to comfort her. "I know, kid. I know," he said, hugging her.

Chapter 13

Around the world—in the major cities and everywhere in between—people cheered as monster-size food stopped falling and the skies began to clear.

The people of Chewandswallow shouted the loudest when the sky over their town was blue and food-free again. Everyone turned their bread boats back to shore.

Tim climbed out, unharmed, from the Port-a-Potty. He looked up at the sky, heart filled with hope as he saw the car-plane approach. He had so much to tell his son! Tim ran to his tackle shop, where a crowd had gathered to greet the heroes.

The crowd went nuts as Manny, Steve, Brent, and Sam emerged from the vehicle. Sam closed the door of the plane, and the townsfolk quickly fell silent.

Tim went up to Sam. "Flint?" he asked softly.

"I'm sorry," she said as a tear rolled down her cheek.

Tim's face fell. "Oh," he muttered.

"Your son was a great man," Sam said.

Just then they all heard loud squawking. Tim and Sam turned to see everyone pointing to a flock of Ratbirds carrying Flint—dazed and smelling of burned food, but very much alive—down to the ground.

After a gentle landing, Flint gave his feathered friends a thumbs-up before they flew away. Then the whole town rushed toward Flint, but Steve got there first.

"Steve!" Flint cried out as he hugged his monkey.

"Flint!" Brent yelled.

"Brent!" Flint called back.

Then Sam came up to Flint. "Flint," she said softly.

"Sam," he replied, overjoyed to see her.

Finally Tim got to his son. "Flint," he said.

"Dad," said Flint.

"Steve," the monkey added.

Tim wanted to pour out his feelings to his son, but he felt very awkward, so he went for what he thought he knew best. "Flint, I, oh . . . when you cast

110

your line . . . if it's not straight . . . you, um–"

Flint was confused.

"Oh, for crying out loud," Sam said, exhausted from watching the two men fumble for the right words. She snatched Steve's Monkey Thought Translator and placed it on Tim's head.

Suddenly Tim was able to tell Flint what he was feeling. "I'm proud of you, Flint," he said. "I'm amazed that someone as ordinary as me could be the father of someone as extraordinary as you. You're talented, you're a total original, and your lab is breathtaking. Your mom–she always knew you were going to be special, and if she were alive today, she'd tell us both, 'I told you so.' Now when I take this thing off and you hear me make a fishing metaphor, just know that fishing metaphors mean"–he took off the translator–"I love my son."

Flint hugged his dad. He had never felt this happy before. "I love you too, Dad."

When Tim stepped away, Flint turned back to Sam.

"So, where were we?" Flint asked her.

"You were about to kiss me," she told him.

"Were you going to kiss me back?" Flint asked.

"Just kiss me," Sam ordered.

And he did.

At that moment Flint's car-plane erupted into flames behind them. Sparks from the explosion rose high into the sky and burst into a bouquet of breathtaking fireworks.

"Yeah! I'm a chicken!" Brent exclaimed.